EDDIE RICKENBACKER

BOY PILOT AND RACER

Written by
Kathryn Cleven Sisson

Illustrated by
Cathy Morrison

Patria Press, Inc.
P.O. Box 752
Carmel, IN 46082
Phone 877–736–7930
Website: www.patriapress.com

Printed and bound in the United States of America
10 9 8 7 6 5 4 3 2 1

Text originally published by the Bobbs-Merrill Company, 1974, in the
Childhood of Famous Americans Series® The Childhood of Famous Americans
Series® is a registered trademark of Simon & Schuster, Inc.

Library of Congress Cataloguing-in-Publication Data

Sisson, Kathryn Cleven, 1904–2002
    Eddie Rickenbacker : boy pilot and racer / written by Kathryn
Cleven Sisson ; illustrated by Cathy Morrison.
    p. cm. — (Young patriots series ; 6)
    "Originally published by the Bobbs-Merrill Company, 1974, in
the Childhood of Famous Americans Series"—T.p. verso.
    Summary: A biography of an automobile racer and pilot who
contributed a great deal towards the growth of military and commercial
aviation in the United States.
    ISBN 1-882859-12-X (hardcover) — ISBN 1-882859-13-8 (pbk.)
    1. Rickenbacker, Eddie, 1890–1973—Childhood and youth
Juvenile literature. 2. Air pilots, Military—United States—Biography
Juvenile literature. [1. Rickenbacker, Eddie, 1890–1973. 2. Air pilots,
Military. 3. Automobile racing drivers.] I. Morrison, Cathy, ill. II. Title.
III. Series.

TL540.R53S5597 2003
629.13'092—dc21
[B]   2002011756

Edited by Harold Underdown
Design by inari

Contents

Illustrations

*This new edition is dedicated to
the memory of the author,
Kathryn Sisson, deceased as of 6 / 13 / 02;
her grandson, Mark C. Engelking,
and her great grandsons,
Richard A. Huckle III, and
Stephen A. Huckle.*

Books in the Young Patriots Series

Watch for more **Young Patriots** Coming Soon
Visit www.patriapress.com for Updates!

Chapter 1

Look Out Eddie!

One afternoon in March 1897, six-year-old Eddie Rickenbacker went to visit his friend Big John in the blacksmith shop. He pumped the long handle of the bellows and watched sparks shoot up from the brick forge. "Slow down there, Eddie," said Big John.

"I'm not really working," said Eddie. "I just want to help you, if I can."

Big John just smiled. Skillfully he picked up a horseshoe with a pair of long tongs and held it in the fire. As soon as it was red hot, he pulled it out and put it on the point of his big iron anvil. "Stand back and watch out for the sparks," he warned.

He struck the hot horseshoe a heavy blow with his hammer. Sparks flew out in all directions, hitting his long leather apron. He pounded the horseshoe again and again, then held it up to look at it.

Big John was preparing this shoe for Duke, the

milkman's horse. The milkman had asked the blacksmith to put new shoes on both front hoofs. Now Duke was hitched a short distance away in the shop. Every few minutes he stamped his foot impatiently on the floor. "Duke doesn't like to wait for his new shoes," said Eddie.

"Well, he'll just have to wait, because it takes time to shape a pair of horseshoes," said Big John.

When he finished shaping the first shoe, he inspected it again, and then plunged it into a tub of cold water. Puffs of steam rose from the tub and clouded the room. "Why do you always put a new shoe in cold water?" asked Eddie.

"One reason is to make it cool so I can handle it with my bare hands," replied Big John. "The other reasons are more difficult to explain."

Eddie now pumped the long handle of the bellows to heat the other horseshoe. Big John hammered it on his anvil and finally plunged it into the tub of water. "They're ready," he said. "Now I'll nail them on Duke's hooves."

He carried both new shoes over to the horse with Eddie following closely. He bent one of Duke's front legs backward so that he could hold the horse's hoof between his knees. Then he began to nail on the shoe.

Eddie stood off at one side and watched. "Could

I make a horseshoe on your forge some day?" he asked, "Sure, but not until you are a few years older," replied Big John.

Just then Eddie's ten-year-old brother Bill appeared, looking impatient. "Come on home, you little scamp!" he cried. "Mama has sent me to get you."

Eddie wanted to stay longer, but if his mother wanted him to come home, he knew he had to go. Solemnly he said good-bye to Big John and followed Bill from the shop.

Bill led the way home across a field covered with a fine layer of snow. As Eddie trudged along, he felt the wet snow soaking through a hole in the sole of one of his shoes. He hurried to get home so he could dry out his foot.

When Bill and Eddie reached their yard, they called to Nanny, a goat tied to a stake in the yard. The Rickenbackers kept Nanny and some other goats for milk. They used goat's milk for drinking and cooking, and sold some in their neighborhood in Columbus, Ohio.

Eddie rushed up the three steps of the back porch of the small Rickenbacker home. He burst into the large kitchen, the only room on the first floor except a bedroom. Upstairs there were two bedrooms where all the older children slept.

By now it was time for supper. Inside the kitchen, Mama was cooking food on the stove and setting the table. She looked at Eddie and cried, "Ach, there you are. Where have you been? It's time to take care of the goats."

Eddie's parents, William and Elizabeth Rickenbacker, had come from Switzerland. They spoke German in their home and so did their children. Two of the other children were older and two younger than Eddie. The two older children were Mary, who helped with many household duties, and William, whom everybody called Bill. Emma was five years old, and Louis was a baby.

"I've been with Big John at the blacksmith shop," he said. "Some day, when I get a little older, he's going to let me use his forge."

"I worry about your going over there," said Mama. "You could get hurt or burned."

"Oh no, Mama," answered Eddie. "I'm always very careful. Big John watches me, and I've learned a lot about his work."

"Huh!" teased Bill, who had just come in from the yard. "Some day, when you grow up, you'll be a genius."

Mary and Mama laughed, and Eddie felt hurt. Quickly he pulled a cap over his reddish hair and ran out to the barn to look after the goats. "Bring

When he bent over to pull the heavy lid back over the
cellar, he suddenly heard the sound of hoof beats.

Mama an egg for the baby," Mary called after him.

"All right," Eddie yelled back.

He carried armfuls of hay for several goats in a
pen near the barn and an armful for Nanny, still
tied in the yard. She playfully nudged him and

bleated out her thanks for the hay.

Next Eddie went to their cellar in the back yard to get the egg for the baby. This cellar was actually a huge hogshead—a kind of barrel—which his father had buried in the ground. It was filled with fruits, vegetables, eggs, and meat, all neatly packed on shelves. The eggs were stored in a jar with a white liquid, called water glass, around them to keep them from spoiling.

Eddie removed the lid from the top of the cellar and climbed down a ladder inside. He trembled with fear because it was dark down in the cellar. Cautiously he reached into the crock, pulled out an egg, and put it into his pocket. Then he wiped the water glass off on his overalls and climbed back up the ladder to the outside.

When he bent over to pull the heavy lid back over the cellar, he suddenly heard the sound of hoof beats. Wham! he went sprawling on the ground. He looked up, and saw Nanny calmly walking away.

At once he thought of the egg in his sweater pocket. Cautiously he reached in his hand and pulled it out, all messy from the broken egg. Angrily he turned to Nanny and shouted, "You mean old goat! I'll get even with you."

By now Papa was home from work and all the members of the family ate supper together. After they finished, Mama sent Bill to get the big family Bible, which was printed in German. Every night after supper she sat at the table and read a few chapters by the light of a kerosene lamp. Then she explained the meaning of what she had read and asked the children to try to lead good lives.

By now the fire in the kitchen stove, which furnished heat for the entire house, was burning low. Mama turned to her husband and said, "William, I need more coal for the cook stove. Our supply is almost gone."

Papa rubbed his black mustache nervously and sighed heavily. "Oh my," he said, "I won't have time tomorrow to get any more coal because I've taken a new job. In the morning I'll have to leave early to start pouring concrete."

"Don't worry, Mama," interrupted Bill. "Tomorrow is Saturday and I won't have to go to school. Eddie and I will go to the railroad tracks and pick up some chunks of coal along the tracks."

"Sure," added Eddie eagerly. He hoped that he would get a chance to see Big John again.

The next morning Bill and Eddie pushed a squeaky wheelbarrow to the railroad tracks. They walked along the tracks and picked up chunks of coal which had rolled off the open coal cars. They played a game to see who could find the most coal.

Moments later the engine stopped, and Eddie fell off,
right on the tracks between the two rails.

Suddenly Bill noticed a switch engine and coal tender coming towards them. "Look out, Eddie," he called.

Eddie stepped back but noticed that the engine and tender were barely moving. Suddenly he was tempted to jump on and take a ride. Happily he ran out and climbed on the back of the tender. Never had he been so thrilled in his life.

Moments later the engine stopped, and Eddie fell off, right on the tracks between the two rails. At first he was too stunned to move, not realizing what had happened. Then as he started to climb to his feet, he discovered, much to his horror, that the engine was starting to back up.

Fortunately Bill was watching. He came and dragged Eddie to one side just as the tender was about to run over him. Then both boys threw themselves on the ground. "You could have been killed," said Bill. "Never do anything like that again."

Eddie knew Bill was right. But he still didn't want his parents to know what had happened. If they did, he'd be kept close to home. It took him the entire walk home for him to get Bill to agree to keep quiet.

Chapter 2

Using His Head

Eddie had many close friends in his neighborhood. They had formed a club, which they called the Horsehead Gang. Nearly every day they worked and played together.

One morning, when Eddie and a few other Horsehead boys were playing, they heard the junkman ringing a cowbell and calling, "Any old iron, old rags, old bones today?"

"That's Sam, the junkman," cried Eddie. "Let's go out to the street to see him."

They saw Sam driving a sway-backed horse hitched to an old wagon. Every few minutes he rang his big rusty cowbell and chanted, "Any old iron, old rags, old bones today?"

A housewife called to Sam and came running out with an old metal coffee pot. Sam weighed the pot on a scale and handed her a few coins. When he reached the spot where the boys were waiting, Eddie suddenly had an idea. "I know where there's lots of old junk around here," he called. "If I bring some of this junk, will you buy it from me?"

"Sure, if you collect the right kinds of junk," replied Sam. Eddie had seen a big iron hinge and a partly buried bone behind a neighbor's barn and ran to get them. "Hey, where are you going?" called the other boys.

"Just wait and you'll soon find out," he replied.

He got the iron hinge and bone and ran back to the street. "Stop, Sam!" he called excitedly. "I have some things for you."

Sam heard him calling and stopped his horse. He climbed down, weighed the hinge and the bone, and tossed them into his wagon. Then he counted out three pennies from a bag. "One, two, three," he said as he placed the pennies in Eddie's out-stretched hand.

"Thank you," said Eddie gratefully.

As he looked at the three pennies he felt very rich. These were the first coins of his own that he had ever had. He felt so rich that he wanted to treat the other Horseheads. "Let's go get some candy," he said.

More than buying candy for his friends, Eddie wanted to earn money to help his parents. For days he carefully searched back yards, alleys and fields, often with the help of some of the Horseheads. He sold what he found to Sam. Finally he proudly gave his mother a handful of pennies. "Thank you, Eddie," she said. "You're a good boy." Then with a twinkle in her eyes she added, "Sometimes."

Soon Eddie began to wonder whether he could trust Sam to weigh things honestly. He noticed that from time to time Sam paid him different numbers of pennies for the same scrap materials. One day he took a basket of scrap metal to a grocery store to have it weighed. It weighed much less on Sam's scale. "I just can't trust Sam," he thought. "He's cheating me in weighing things."

He soon thought of a way to take care of this problem. He ran to talk with his mother, who was hoeing the garden. "Mama," he asked anxiously, "will you lend me twenty-five cents?"

Mama looked up in surprise and pushed her sunbonnet back from her hot forehead. "You want to borrow twenty-five cents? I don't understand. What do you want to buy?"

"I want to buy a second-hand scale," replied Eddie. "I know where I can get one for twenty-five cents."

"I still don't understand," said Mama. "Why do you want to buy a scale?"

The next morning he carried his brass and bones out to
the street and waited for Sam to come by.

"Because I think Sam cheats me when he
weighs pieces of junk," answered Eddie. "I want to
weigh things in advance so he can't cheat me any
longer. If you'll lend me the twenty-five cents, I'll
make enough more to pay you back."

Mama hesitated, but soon agreed. "Yes, I'll lend

you the money," she said, "but first you'll have to help me finish hoeing the garden."

Eddie ran fast to the shed and picked out a hoe. Carefully he went along the rows of vegetables, chopping out weeds, glad that he had such an understanding mother.

After he finished hoeing, he hurried off to buy the scale. Back home he weighed some brass and bones which he planned to sell to Sam. "According to my scale, I have twenty pounds here," he said. "Now I wonder how much Sam's scale will say I have."

The next morning he carried his brass and bones out to the street and waited for Sam to come by. Soon he heard Sam ringing his cowbell and calling out, "Any old iron, old rags, old bones today?"

As usual, Sam greeted him in a friendly manner. He climbed down from his wagon and weighed Eddie's collection. "Fifteen pounds," he announced, and he started to throw the stuff into his wagon.

"Just a minute," cried Eddie. He ran back to the house, snatched up his scale, and brought it back out to the street. Sam looked at the scale in surprise.

Eddie started to weigh his collection. "My scale says that I have twenty pounds. That's five pounds more than your scale says."

Sam scarcely knew what to say or do. He nervously scratched his short gray beard. "There must be something wrong with your scale," he said.

"Oh, no," replied Eddie. "I'm sure it's right because I checked it with the scale at the grocery store. You owe me for twenty pounds."

"Well, I won't argue with you," said Sam, handing him the right number of coins.

From then on, Eddie never had any problems with Sam about how much his scrap weighed. They became very close friends.

Chapter 3

Secondhand Clothes
for School

Later that year, Eddie started going to school at the East Main Street Public School in Columbus. At first he had a hard time, because he had always spoken German with his family. In school, he was supposed to speak, read, and write in English. One day he explained his problem to his mother and said, "Mama, why can't we speak English here at home? Then maybe I won't have so much trouble at school."

"I'll speak to Papa about it when he comes home," said Mama. "He probably will be willing, if it will help you in school."

That evening she explained the matter to Papa and they decided to speak English part of the time at home. This change helped Eddie, but English was still difficult for him.

Late one afternoon shortly after school had started, the firebell rang furiously in the hall. "Get in line for a fire drill!" ordered the teacher, rushing to the door.

Quickly and quietly under her directions the children formed a line and marched outside. At once they became excited because they could see smoke coming out of the basement windows. Within a few minutes they heard the clang, clang of the fire engine coming down the street. Soon a red fire engine arrived, pulled by galloping horses. The firemen jumped off and pulled a fire hose toward the basement.

Eddie watched closely and danced about with excitement. Then suddenly he remembered his coat and cap, still inside his classroom. At once, without saying a word, he dashed through the front door of the building.

Inside the hall, he found his way blocked by a sheet of flames shooting upward. He hesitated for a moment, and then leaped through them. The heat almost strangled him and scorched his hair, but he kept on going. He rushed into the classroom and grabbed his coat and cap. Holding them tightly, he dashed through the flames again to the door.

Once he got outside, he realized the great risk he had taken by going back into the burning build-

He rushed into the classroom and
grabbed his coat and cap.

ing. He trembled with fear and took off for home, running all the way. When he reached the back steps, he slumped down, completely exhausted.

After he recovered his breath, he went inside and told his mother what he had done. "Oh, no!" she exclaimed. "You might have been burned to death. Why did you do it?"

"Well," said Eddie, "I need my coat and cap. They are the only ones I have good enough to wear to school. I just couldn't take a chance on losing them."

The following summer the Rickenbackers had very little money. Papa earned just a small amount doing cement work about the city. When fall came, he and Mama had to buy second-hand clothes for the children to wear to school.

Eddie's second-hand shoes didn't match. His left shoe was brown with a square toe, and his right shoe was yellow with a pointed toe. "Hey, Papa," he cried. "They don't match. Do I have to wear them to school?"

"I'm afraid so," replied his father. "They were the only shoes left in your size."

Eddie was worried that the other students would make fun of him for wearing these shoes. They already called him "Dutchy" because he spoke with a German accent. "Now they'll start teasing me all over again," he said.

"I'm sorry, son," said Papa, patting him on the shoulder. "When things get better, I'll buy you a pair of shoes that match."

The next day at school, as Eddie had expected, the children made fun of his shoes. "Look at Dutchy's funny shoes," they called, "with a brown square-toed shoe on one foot and a yellow pointed-toe shoe on the other."

This teasing made him so angry that he felt he would explode. He chased the children, but they only teased him all the harder. "Left foot, yellow bright, right foot, what a sight," they called as they ran from him.

To help their family, both Eddie and Bill did many chores at home. They brought coal and wood for the kitchen stove and carried water from the well near the barn to use in the kitchen. They fed, watered, and milked the goats, fed the chickens, and gathered the eggs. Every now and then they got out tools to make simple repairs around the house. Papa had taught them how to use and take care of tools.

Eddie was always eager to make things with tools. One day when he went to the blacksmith shop, Big John let him make a horseshoe, as he had promised he would when Eddie was older. Eddie pumped the bellows to heat the shoe and hammered it on the anvil. When he finished, Big John carefully examined it and said, "You've done a mighty good job."

One evening in February 1898, Papa came home from work carrying a newspaper with a big black headline, which read, "Battleship Maine Blown Up in Cuba." He pointed to the headline and said, "This is something serious. It could lead to a war between the United States and Spain."

"War?" asked Eddie in surprise. He still was too young to understand what a war was like, but he knew that it was something terrible in which men fought to kill one another.

"Yes," replied Papa. "Spain took a big chance in blowing up our battleship. We might declare war on Spain."

"Why are we having trouble with Spain?" asked Bill. "That country is way across the Atlantic Ocean in Europe."

"We have to know some history for the answer," said Papa. "Columbus, who discovered America, came from Spain. Following his discovery, Spain claimed and settled many places in America, including Cuba and Puerto Rico. They have ruled both these islands ever since, but now the people in Cuba want freedom. They are fighting for independence."

"Do you mean that they want to be free from Spain just like the American colonies wanted to be free from England?" asked Bill.

"Yes. Our government has told Spain to set Cuba free, but the rebellion goes on," replied Papa. "Now Spain may claim that we had no right to have our battleship tied up in a Cuban harbor. On the other hand, we probably will accuse Spain of blowing up the battleship without a just cause."

About two months later, the United States declared war on Spain. President McKinley called for 125,000 volunteer soldiers to fight in the war. Big headlines in newspapers proclaimed the news in all parts of the country.

A few evenings later, Papa pushed away his half-empty plate and sat nervously stroking his black mustache. He looked around at his children, who now included young Dewey and a new baby, Albert. Finally he said, "I have something to say. America has been very good to me, and I'm thankful to have such a fine family. President McKinley has called for volunteers to help fight a war with Spain. I don't like war, but I feel that I owe it to my country to enlist."

Mama and all the children gasped in surprise. Eddie glanced in her direction and noticed tears trickling down her cheeks. Some of the children started to ask questions, but Papa raised his hands to silence them. "Let us hear from Mama first," he said.

Smiling proudly through her tears, Mama said, "This is a noble idea, William. You owe it to America to enlist. We'll miss you but will manage to get along while you are away."

The next day, which was Saturday, Papa left on a horse-drawn streetcar for the army recruiting station. He planned to return later in the day to bid his family farewell and to get a few things to take with him.

The children could hardly wait for him to come back. They wanted to be sure to be there to say good-bye. A couple of hours later, they saw him coming and rushed out to meet him. "Hello, Papa," they called. "Are you a soldier now? Have you enlisted for war?"

Papa merely shook his head and hurried into the house. Mama rushed out from the bedroom where she had been taking care of the baby. "What's the news?" she asked eagerly. "Have you enlisted? Are you going to leave?"

"No," Papa said. "The recruiting officers wouldn't take me. They explained that they couldn't take fathers with seven children. I guess they think that fathers like me are needed at home. So I won't be going away."

"Hurrah!" shouted the children, joining hands and dancing around him merrily.

Papa went back to work and soon made enough money to buy Eddie a new pair of shoes. "I really have a great father," he said proudly to some of his friends at school. "He even tried to enlist in the army to help our country fight this war against Spain."

The Spanish-American War lasted only a few months. The United States Army and Navy won several fierce battles and Spain gave up. Then the two countries signed a treaty, and the short war was over—not that Eddie cared. He had many more important things to think about and do.

Chapter 4

Daily Mixture of Work and Fun

After his first year of school, Eddie had to spend a lot of time during the summer vacation looking after the goats, because Bill had a job for the summer. Every day he had to find a good place for them to pasture. He usually walked ahead with Nanny, and the other goats followed. She was one of the oldest goats in the herd, and the others depended on her as a leader. Their herd was growing; Nanny and a few other goats had baby goats, or kids.

One morning when Eddie was taking the goats to pasture, one of the Horsehead boys came to join him "Where are you going?" he asked

Eddie pointed to a thicket along a nearby stream. "Over there, where they can nibble on the twigs and leaves and drink water from the stream," he replied.

"What are you going to do next?" asked the Horsehead boy. "Can you come play later this morning?"

"No," replied Eddie. "When I get back from taking the goats to pasture, I'll have to deliver goat's milk to our neighbors. I take the money for the milk home to my mother. She needs every cent she can get to buy groceries for us."

That morning Bill had helped to milk the goats before he left for work. He and Eddie had taken some of the milk to the house for Mama to use and had put the rest in two-gallon cans. When Eddie set off to deliver milk, he pushed the cans along in a little cart. He knocked at a kitchen door and called "Good morning. Here's your goat's milk. How much do you want this morning?"

The neighbor woman stepped out the door with a pitcher in her hands. "I'll take a quart this morning," she said.

Eddie poured a quart of milk into her pitcher and she handed him a nickel. "I'll take another quart tomorrow," she said.

When Eddie reached the next house, he found the woman already at the door, waiting for him. "Give me two quarts," she said. "Your goat's milk will be good for my sick baby. Bring me another quart tomorrow."

Eddie kept on going along the street until he sold his milk. Then he rushed back to the thicket to check on the goats. When he arrived, he found some of his Horsehead friends waiting for him. They were trying to keep a strange tan and white dog from chasing some of the goats. One boy grabbed a stone to throw at the dog. "Don't chase her away," called Eddie.

He whistled softly to the dog, and she came close to him and sniffed his hand. He patted her and she started to jump on him as if to make friends. "She's dirty and hungry," he said to the other boys. "I think I'll take her home and feed her and give her a bath. Then maybe my parents will let me keep her."

When he reached home with the dog, he took her to the barn to keep her out of sight. "I'll give her some goat's milk to drink and wash her with soap and water before I let my parents see her," he said. "Then if they let me keep her, I'll call her Trixie."

Eddie's parents reminded him that somebody might come to claim the dog but promised him that if nobody came, he could keep her. After several days of waiting, he decided that she really belonged to him.

During the summer Eddie did have time to play marbles with the other Horsehead boys. He nearly always won and they began to call him

"Champ." This made him very happy because he felt jealous of his brother Bill, who was the champion player at school.

One Saturday afternoon when Bill came home from work, Eddie said, "Let's play a game of marbles. I'm champion of the Horseheads, and I think I can beat you."

Bill laughed. He hadn't played marbles since school had let out several weeks ago, but he felt certain that he could win. "Sure, I'll play," he said.

They went out into the back yard and marked off a large circle with the toes of their shoes. In the center of the circle they made a smaller circle with a straight line across it. Then each shot a marble toward the line to see who would start the game. Eddie's marble stopped right on the straight line in the center, so he won the right to play first in the game.

They counted out an equal number of marbles and placed them in the form of a cross in the center circle. Some of their marbles were made of stone, some of glass, and others of metal. Each boy would get to keep all the marbles he could shoot out of the outer circle with a marble called a shooter. "Go ahead," Bill called confidently.

"All right," said Eddie, kneeling at the edge of the outer circle. He held his shooter on the ground and carefully shot it toward the cross of marbles in the center. It hit the marbles just right and made one of them roll out of the circle. "Good!" cried Eddie. "Now I get another shot."

He aimed again, holding his breath in suspense. Bing! His shooter knocked another marble out of the circle. He kept on shooting until he had knocked eight marbles out of the circle. This was more than Bill could stand. "Come on and miss," he cried. "Give me a chance to play."

Eddie kept right on winning until he knocked all the marbles from the ring. Happily he reached down to pick up the last marble. "Do you want to play any more?" he asked.

"Sure," said Bill, going for more marbles. "You're not as good as you think you are."

In a few minutes, Eddie won again. "Now do you agree that I'm champ?" he asked.

By now Bill was too angry to answer. He jumped on Eddie and the two boys started to wrestle on the ground. Bill had the advantage because he was much larger and stronger. Suddenly Trixie came running. She jumped into the fray and bit Bill on the leg. "She bit me!" he shouted fiercely.

Angrily he jumped to his feet and started to kick at Trixie. She dodged his kicks and kept barking and jumping at him. Papa heard the

Suddenly Trixie came running. She jumped into the
fray and bit Bill on the leg.

noise and came running into the yard, shouting "Ach! Stop this racket!"

Trixie now left Bill and started to jump on Papa, barking and snarling. She grabbed him by the legs of his trousers, and he kicked to shake her loose. Soon she stopped attacking him and ran back to Eddie. "By golly," exclaimed Papa, "you sure are safe with a fighter like her around to protect you."

Near the Rickenbacker house there was a gravel pit, which regularly closed each Saturday noon for the weekend. One Saturday afternoon, when they could look around as much as they wanted, the Horseheads decided to visit the pit. At the bottom of the pit there was a small steel car, which the workmen used to haul gravel up to the top to be loaded into wagons. The car ran on rails and was pulled by a cable up a steep bank.

The boys thought it would be fun to roll the car up the rails to the top. The older boys pushed the car inch by inch, and Eddie followed along behind, putting chunks of wood behind the wheels to keep it from rolling backwards. They could barely move the car, but they thought they were having fun.

When they had almost reached the top, the older boys climbed into the car to rest. Eddie decided that it would be fun to kick the chunks of wood out from under the wheels and let the car roll backward. "Here goes nothing!" he shouted as he kicked the chunks out of the way and jumped into the car.

The car started downward like a flash, jumped the rails and flipped over. It threw all the boys out, but Eddie was the only one hurt. A wheel ran over one of his legs and cut the flesh to the bone.

All the older boys rushed to help him. They dragged him up out of the pit and half carried him home. When his mother first saw his bleeding leg, she cried, "Oh, no, Eddie, won't you ever learn?"

One evening after Eddie's leg had healed, he and his father sat on the back porch. Earlier they had put all the goats in a pen in back of the barn for the night. Suddenly they heard old Nanny let out a loud bleat. Eddie ran fast to see what was the trouble and found a big dog attacking her. Quick as a flash he grabbed the big dog and tried to pull him away. The dog turned on him and almost knocked him down.

Moments later Papa reached the pen. He picked up a stick of wood and whacked the dog a few times to drive it away. "Are you all right, son?" he asked.

"Yes, I'm all right, but is Nanny?" said Eddie.

"Yes," said his father, taking Eddie's hand and leading him back to the house. "You took a big risk in grabbing that dog. Never do anything like that again."

"What should I have done?" asked Eddie in a puzzled tone of voice. "I couldn't stand by and let that big dog kill old Nanny."

"No, but it would have been better for him to kill Nanny than to kill you," said Papa. "From now on, try to think before you act."

Chapter 5

The Circus Parade

On the last day of school in the spring of 1900, Eddie rushed home from school. "A circus is coming to town, Mama," he cried. "Men are putting posters all over town. Can we go? It will only cost fifty cents."

Mama bit her lip and shook her head. "I'm afraid not," she replied, "because we need every penny we can scrape up to make a payment on the house."

At once Eddie felt guilty about asking his mother to spend money on a circus. His sister Mary had to work in a factory to help support the family. "I understand, Mama," he said, "but maybe we can go to the parade. There'll be a big free parade downtown. Do you think we can go?"

"Yes, I'm sure we can," said his mother. "I've never seen a circus parade and I'd like to see one. Maybe I can find enough nickels for us to ride downtown on the horse streetcar."

Eddie let out one of his wildest Horsehead yells. "Ride on the horse streetcar?" he shouted. "What a day that will be!"

He could hardly wait for the day to come. When it did, he got up extra early to get dressed. He put on his best knickers and a clean shirt which his mother had just washed and ironed. He also put on shoes and socks, instead of going barefoot, as he usually did at home.

Besides Eddie, Mama took Emma and Louis to the parade. She arranged to leave the two youngest children with a neighbor. The two older children, Mary and Bill, couldn't go because they were working.

Mama and the three children waited at the corner for the horse streetcar. Soon two horses came into sight, pulling the big car along the middle of the street. "Here it comes," shouted Eddie.

The car was open on both sides, with rows of benches inside. At first, some of the benches were empty, but soon all of them were filled. Then people hung onto the sides of the car.

Downtown, the sidewalks and curbs were packed with people waiting to see the parade. Mama found them an open place by the curb where the children could see. Soon two of Eddie's Horsehead friends called to him. They had climbed up on a fence along the sidewalk. "Hey, Eddie," they shouted. "Come up here with us."

Eddie wanted to join them, but he knew he should stay with Mama. "I can't," he shouted, "but I'll see you later."

Before long the blaring of band music could be heard in the distance. "Something's coming!" cried Louis. "I hear music."

When Eddie got his first look at the parade, he could hardly believe his eyes. A horseless carriage or automobile chugged along at the head of the parade. He had heard of these, but had never seen one before. It puffed and belched out smelly black smoke, but it kept moving all by itself. This horseless carriage had a single seat, wooden wheels, and narrow rubber tires. A man sat on one seat and steered it with a long lever. A sign, which hung on one side, read, "The Duryea, winner of America's first auto race at the amazing speed of seven miles per hour."

Right behind the horseless carriage came the bandwagon, pulled by prancing gray horses. This wagon was painted bright red and blue with gold trimming. All the members of the band sat up high on the wagon and wore bright-colored uniforms.

Next came men and women in colorful costumes

riding prancing white horses. Trudging along behind came fire swallowers and ropewalkers and funny-faced clowns. Then came a group of Indians riding spotted ponies. After the Indians came wild animals in cages mounted on wagons pulled by horses. In some of the cages golden lions and striped tigers could be seen showing their teeth. Colorful birds flew about in other cages, and in still others monkeys performed tricks. Plodding along behind the cages came camels with their heads high in the air. Behind the camels came a herd of forty elephants, all stepping along in orderly fashion. "Oh, here come the elephants!" cried Eddie. "How big they look!"

"Let me see," wailed Louis, as people crowded around him. "I want to see." Eddie and Emma held him up so that he could see better.

Last came a gold and red wagon with a row of big pipes sticking up from it. A woman at the keyboard in front of them played ear-splitting music. As she played, steam puffed from the pipes. "That's a calliope," Mama explained to Eddie. "It's a kind of steam musical instrument."

As the calliope passed most people clapped their hands over their ears. Eddie loved it, however, and hated to see it leave because it brought the end of the parade. When they left for home, he felt that this had been the most exciting day of his life.

The next morning Eddie and the Horseheads talked excitedly about the parade. They spent most of their time talking about the horseless carriage. Finally Eddie said, "Let's make one."

"What do you mean?" asked the other boys. "How can we make a horseless carriage?"

"Well, of course our horseless carriage won't run by itself," replied Eddie. "We can sit in it and steer it, but we'll need somebody to push it. Maybe we could call it a pushmobile instead of an automobile."

"Where will we get the wheels for it?" asked one of the boys.

"We'll make them," replied Eddie.

He took them to his father's workshop, where they sawed out wheels from a wide board. While they were working on the wheels, he found pieces of old water pipe to use for axles. They mounted the wheels on the axles and put a wide board across the axles to hold them in place. Finally they tied ropes to the ends of the front axles to use for steering.

After they finished the pushmobile, they stood and admired it. Several boys sat on the wide board and pretended to be driving it. "Now let's take it out and test it," said Eddie. "The guys who push it the hardest and steer it the best will win."

Finally they tied ropes to the ends of the front
axles to use for steering.

At first they had a hard time finding a place to
drive their new toy. Eddie suggested building a
special racetrack in the field in back of his father's
barn. "Maybe we can get other boys to help us," he
said. "If they want to build pushmobiles, we can
have races. What do you guys think?"

"That's a good idea," cried the others. "Let's get
going."

They easily found several groups of boys who

wanted to build pushmobiles too. They all worked together, cutting down trees, mowing grass, and moving dirt to build a smooth track around the field. Several days later they finished the new track.

The boys held a meeting to plan the first race. "We have to have some money so we can give prizes," said Eddie. "Everybody has to pay a penny to enter the race, and everybody who comes to watch it has to pay a penny."

From then on the boys had many exciting pushmobile races. Sometimes they tried so hard to win that they argued and had free-for-all fights. The pushers tried to bump one another and the drivers to cause collisions.

Eddie had fun with the others, but he wasn't satisfied. He wanted to build a pushmobile that would run easier and faster. One day he noticed an empty baby buggy with ballbearing wheels standing in front of a neighbor's house. He pushed it a little way and was surprised by how easily it rolled. Without thinking he started to run, pushing it as fast as he could.

Suddenly the neighbor noticed that her baby buggy was gone. She rushed out of the house shrieking angrily at Eddie. "Stop running away with my baby buggy!" she called. "Bring it back immediately."

Eddie, caught by surprise, looked back and saw

the angry woman coming toward him. "I'm sorry," he said, shoving the baby buggy toward her and running away. He hid behind the nearest barn and went home cautiously.

Eddie was sure that he had made an important discovery. Ball-bearing wheels would make a push-mobile move easier and faster. Now he had to find two axles with ball-bearing wheels, but this would be hard to do because ball-bearing wheels were new. Finally he thought of Sam the junkman. "I'll ask him to find me some," he said to himself.

He knew that Sam actually handled only old junk. But he felt sure that somehow Sam could find two axles with ball-bearing wheels.

Chapter 6

Pushmobile Racers

On Friday, Eddie waited impatiently for Sam the junkman to come along. Soon he heard him ringing his cowbell and calling, "Any old iron, old rags, old bones today?" Quickly Eddie explained his problem, and Sam said, "I'll see what I can do."

One week later, Sam returned, proudly holding up two axles with ball-bearing wheels. "Here they are, Eddie," he called. "I hope you can use them."

"Oh, thanks!" said Eddie. "They're just what I need. How much do I owe you?"

"Not a thing," replied Sam.

"I don't owe you anything for getting them for me?"

"That's right," said Sam. "I just want to help you build a pushmobile fast enough to win many races."

Eddie immediately started to build a new pushmobile with which to surprise the boys at the next race. To keep it secret, he hid the pushmobile in a corner of the barn and threw an old canvas over it. He arranged secretly for the best pusher in the neighborhood to push it for him. If he won, he would share his prize with the pusher.

On race day, all the boys stared in surprise at Eddie's new pushmobile. The drivers lined up for the race and started with loud whoops. Eddie shot past all the other drivers, and none could catch up with him. "We've won!" he shouted to his pusher as they came in first in the race.

He jumped off, grabbed his pusher and swung him round and round. "We went like greased lightning, maybe a mile a minute," he exclaimed. Then he patted the pushmobile and added, "I'll call it 'Mile-a-Minute-Murphy' after the famous bicycle racer."

At that time Charles Murphy, the bicycle racer, was the talk of the country. He had set a world record by riding a mile in one minute. This was the first time anybody had made a bike go such an amazing speed.

Sometimes Eddie and the Horseheads went to watch bicycle races, and he admired the riders for their strength and skill. He learned that a person had to keep fit to compete in any kind of racing.

"Some day I want to be a bicycle racer," he thought. "From now on I'll save every penny I can to buy a second-hand bicycle. Maybe Sam can find one for me."

That summer Eddie had to do more chores than usual because Bill had a job away from home. He again had to look after the herd of goats, which now was much larger, and had to deliver more goat's milk to their customers. He had to take care of the chickens and bring both water and fuel to the kitchen.

He still found time to earn money on the side. He made a few pennies here and there by running errands or doing odd jobs for neighbors. Finally he asked Sam to find him an old bicycle, but it came with a twisted frame. "I'll take it to John at the blacksmith shop," he said, "and ask him to help me fix it. I'm sure he can bend it back into shape."

Big John was happy to help him straighten the frame. When he reached home, it was almost as good as new. During the next few days he had great fun riding it along the streets with Trixie chasing him.

At the same time a bicycle rider named Knabenshue was traveling about the country in a big balloon called a dirigible. When he came to Columbus, Eddie and some of his friends went to watch him land. They stood spellbound as they looked up at the big dirigible floating through the air. "Hey, guys," cried Eddie, "would you like to be floating in that thing up there?"

"Oh, no," replied his friends. "It's too scary for us."

"Not for me," replied Eddie. "I wouldn't be afraid at all. Some day I hope I'll be able to fly about high in the air."

"How?" asked his friends.

"I don't know," replied Eddie, "but I'll find a way."

That night after he went to bed he lay awake, trying to think of a way to fly. Soon he came up with the idea of buying a large umbrella he had seen at a second-hand store. Then he would fasten the open umbrella to his bicycle and ride off the roof of a barn.

The next morning he told the neighbor boys about his plan. "I'll take off from our neighbor's barn," he said. "It has a steep roof, and I'll need all the speed I can get."

The other boys looked at him doubtfully. "What if your plan doesn't work?" they asked. "Won't you need a soft place to land?"

"Yes, just for safety I'll prepare a soft landing place back of the barn," replied Eddie. "Maybe you guys can help me bring some sand from the gravel pit to pile on the ground."

Down the sloping roof he rolled, and shot off into the air.

"You bet," said the boys. "We'll do anything to help you fly."

The boys made several trips to the gravel pit and built a large sandpile in back of the barn. Then Eddie asked one of the boys to help him take the bicycle and umbrella up to the roof of the barn. He tied the handle of the open umbrella to the frame of the bicycle.

He and his friend soon had the bicycle and open umbrella on the ridge of the roof, and he climbed onto the seat of the bicycle. Down below his friends cheered him and Trixie looked up at him and barked. He waved back at them and felt a bit afraid as he saw how far it was to the ground. "Let's go," he said to his friend. "I might as well get started."

Down the sloping roof he rolled, and shot off into the air. The big umbrella turned inside out and he fell straight down to the sandpile. Quickly Trixie ran up to lick his face and all the boys gathered around to see if he was hurt. "Are you all right?" they cried anxiously.

"I guess so," he said sadly as he slowly got to his feet.

Their neighbor heard the commotion behind her barn and ran out to see what had happened. Angrily she ordered the boys to leave and helped Eddie to limp home. "What a foolish thing for him to do," she told Mama. "It's a wonder he wasn't killed. He must never jump off the roof of my barn again."

Mama was angry, too, but Eddie noticed a tear in her eye. "Tell me, Eddie," she scolded, "why did you ever do such a foolish thing?"

"I'm sorry, Mama," he replied. "I was only trying to find out if I could fly."

"Well, please promise not to do such a silly thing again," she said. "Why, it's so silly that I can hardly believe you did it."

"I promise, Mama," he replied. By now he could hardly believe it himself.

Chapter 7

Torchlight Parade for a President

Late one September afternoon, Eddie lay on his stomach in the front yard, looking for a four-leaf clover. He had heard that finding a four-leaf clover would bring a person good luck. "What are you doing over there?" called his father.

"I'm looking for a four-leaf clover," he said. "But so far I haven't been able to find one."

"Ach, is that all you have to do?" asked Papa, shaking his head. "You can find more important things to do than that."

"Well, I've already fed the goats and put them in the pen back of the barn," said Eddie. "While they are eating I thought I might find a four-leaf clover."

"Forget that foolish stuff, son," said Papa, starting on toward the house. "You can't find luck. You make it."

Eddie climbed to his feet and put his hands deep in his overall pockets. "Maybe Papa is right," he thought. "I should make my own good luck instead of trying to find it."

Later at the supper table, when Papa finished eating, he pushed back his plate and looked across the table at Eddie and Bill. "How would you boys like to go downtown with me tonight to see a torchlight parade for President William H. McKinley?" he asked. "The President is coming to Columbus to campaign for election to another four-year term."

"Oh, great!" cried Bill. "I want to go."

"So do I," said Eddie excitedly. "Today I saw a big picture of President McKinley on a building downtown. Is he really a great President?"

"Yes, I think he is," replied Papa. "He helped our country to win a quick victory in the war with Spain and he has helped working people to have better times. I'm getting along better with my work and making more money."

"I know," agreed Mama. "We have more money to spend on food and clothes."

"That's right," said Papa, looking across the table. "For some time you have wanted me to build an addition to the house. Well, the way things are going, I think I can afford to build a couple of rooms this fall."

Mama's face flushed with happiness. "Now we won't have to stay in the kitchen all the time."

In a few minutes Papa and the two boys boarded a horse-drawn streetcar to go downtown. As they rode along Eddie said, "Today when I saw the picture of President McKinley there was a picture of another man beside him and it said, 'Elect McKinley and Roosevelt.' What is Mr. Roosevelt running for?"

"That was Theodore Roosevelt, who is running for Vice-President with President McKinley," explained Papa. "He was a colonel in the Spanish-American War, and won an important battle."

"Will he be in the parade tonight with President McKinley?" asked Eddie.

"No, I don't think so," replied Papa. "He probably is campaigning tonight in some other part of the country."

When Papa and the boys arrived downtown, they saw a big banner reading, "Welcome President McKinley" over the street. The sidewalks were crowded with people waiting for the parade to start. Some were looking out of high windows and some were even hanging onto electric light poles to see.

A drummer boy came first, followed by some boys blowing horns. Next came columns of men carrying lighted torches which flashed and flickered in the

A drummer boy came first, followed by
some boys blowing horns.

darkness. After them came several brass bands with
men in fancy uniforms playing lively music. Groups
of men carrying signs urging people to vote for
McKinley and Roosevelt walked between the bands.
One sign which Papa especially liked read, "Vote for

four more years with a full dinner pail."

Last in the parade came President McKinley, riding in a carriage drawn by four high-stepping bay horses. Every now and then he bowed and waved to the people, and they shouted wildly in return. "He certainly looks like a great man," Eddie said to Bill as they stared admiringly at the carriage.

The parade ended at the state capitol building in the center of the city. The President left his carriage and climbed the broad steps of the building to make a speech. The torchbearers, bands, and people from the streets all poured onto the statehouse grounds and crowded around to listen. Eddie thought that he never had spent such an exciting evening in his life.

That fall, Eddie felt that he was old enough to get a job somewhere to begin to earn money. "Maybe I can get a job delivering papers," he said to himself. One day he walked two miles downtown to the offices of a newspaper. He got a morning newspaper route that paid a dollar a week. "You'll have to come early in the morning every day to pick up your papers," said the man. "Can we count on your being here on time?"

Eddie quickly thought over the work he would have to do before going to school. First he would have to deliver his papers and afterwards do all his chores. "Yes, sir," he replied. "I'll be here on time every morning."

During the following months, he trudged to the newspaper office before daylight each morning to pick up newspapers to deliver on his route. Many people praised him for delivering their papers early so they could read them before they went to work.

In late spring, he heard of a job picking strawberries. This job would last only a few weeks, but he could make much more money each week than he was making on the paper route. He took this job, but it was extremely boring. Many times he wished he was back delivering papers again.

He found other things to do that did interest him. One day Eddie discovered that a pair of robins had built a nest in one of the trees in the back yard. After the eggs hatched, Eddie dug up worms to give to the robins for their babies. He watched them grow and even gave them scraps of food.

One Sunday morning after Eddie had dressed for church, he decided to go out and check on the robins before he left. As he looked up, he saw a big gray cat on the limb near the baby robins in their nest. "Hey, you old cat!" he called. "Come down from there."

The cat simply crawled closer and stared at the baby robins. Trixie came and barked, and Eddie tried to frighten the cat by throwing a stick near it. The cat fell, landing on his head. Trixie jumped up on him trying to reach the cat—and the two adult robins flew down, trying to chase it away.

Almost immediately the cat leaped to the ground and ran fast for the barn, with Trixie chasing it. Then the two robins flew up to their baby birds in the nest. Once more everything was calm and peaceful in the back yard. Eddie reached up to rub the scratches on his head and went on to church. "How lucky I was to come out here when I did," he thought.

Chapter 8

No Lightning But Still Alive

T hunder rumbled and lightning flashed across the sky. Twelve-year-old Eddie sat in his seat at school reading about Benjamin Franklin. He read that Franklin had flown a kite during a thunderstorm to discover that lightning was a form of electricity. As Eddie read, he had an exciting idea. He would make a kite and try to get electricity from lightning too.

After school he hurried home to his father's workshop in the barn. He picked out two sticks to nail together for the framework. Now he needed silk cloth to cover it, just as Franklin had used. Also, he needed some copper wire, which he planned to use instead of string for flying the kite because it would conduct electricity easily. He soon thought of Sam the junkman.

The next time Sam came by, Eddie rushed out front to see him. He explained what he was trying to do and asked Sam if he had any silk and any copper wire. Sam lifted his derby hat and scratched his gray beard thoughtfully. "Yes, I think I can help you," he said.

He pulled out a bundle of old clothes he had just purchased. Inside he found an old silk shirt that was just what Eddie needed. "Oh, great!" cried Eddie. "I knew you could help me."

Sam reached into his cart, and pulled out a roll of fine copper wire. "Is this about the kind of wire you want?" he asked.

"That's exactly the kind I need," replied Eddie. "Now, how much do I owe you for the shirt and the wire?"

"Not a thing," answered Sam. "I just hope you have luck in using them to catch some electricity from lightning."

"Oh, thanks, Sam," called Eddie, rushing back to his father's workshop.

Carefully he cut out a big piece of silk from the old shirt and fastened it to the cross pieces of his kite. At the top of the framework he put a straight piece of copper wire to help attract electricity. At the bottom of the framework he fastened a short tail, made out of small pieces of the silk shirt.

Happily he took his kite out back of the barn and waited
for lightning to begin to flash overhead.

Finally he fastened the long thin copper wire to the kite to use in flying it and in pulling it down. At the end of the wire where he would be holding it, he tied an old key, just as Benjamin Franklin had done in flying his kite.

Soon another thunderstorm approached the city. Happily he took his kite out back of the barn and waited for lightning to begin to flash overhead. When he thought the right moment had come, he tossed the kite into the air and watched it float upward gracefully to the clouds. Then every time the lightning flashed, he looked for a spark of electricity on the key, but nothing happened.

Soon it began to rain, and he stepped back into the barn doorway, being careful to keep the kite up in the clouds. He held his knuckles close to the key, just as Franklin had done, but still felt no signs of electricity. "What's wrong?" he asked himself. "I've tried to do everything just right."

The thunderstorm moved on and Eddie, disappointed and puzzled, hauled in his kite. "I'll tell my teacher about my experiment and ask her what was wrong," he thought. "I'm sure she can tell me."

The next day he told his teacher all about his experiment. "Oh, my!" she exclaimed. "You should have used string instead of copper wire to fly the kite. If the kite had attracted any electricity it might have run down the copper wire and killed you."

Eddie swallowed hard and looked at her. "Oh!" he cried. "I didn't know."

"Yes," explained his teacher, "that's really a dangerous experiment. The lightning killed the first person that tried it after Franklin. You're lucky to be alive."

"Well, now you have told me these things, I won't try it again," said Eddie.

About this time Eddie's father became the foreman of a bridge-building company. Eddie often went with him to watch the men build a bridge. Once when they were building a bridge across a river, Papa said, "Pioneer wagons crossed this river on rafts to help settle our country. Now we're building this bridge so that horses can pull carriages and wagons across. Ach, before long some of those horseless carriages will cross here."

Eddie nodded to agree with Papa. "My father really is proud of what he is doing," he thought. "By building bridges like this, he's helping to build a better America."

Eddie wanted to build too, and one day at school, he read that people had tried to build a perpetual motion machine, a machine that would make its own power and run forever. "I think I'll try to make one myself," he said.

That evening Eddie went to his father's work-shop. Gradually he put together a device in which wooden balls served as weights to make wheels turn. One wooden ball would make a wheel turn and lift another wooden ball, which would make a second wheel to turn and lift still another wooden ball, and so on.

One evening when Papa was going to work on a bridge at night, he stopped at the workshop to see what Eddie was doing. Proudly Eddie showed him his new machine and said, "This machine will make me a fortune, Papa. I'll be as famous as Barney Oldfield, the bike racer."

Papa watched the wooden balls in the device go up and make the wheels go around. At last he said, "It seems to work all right, but what good is it?"

"What good is it?" repeated Eddie, surprised.

"Yes, what will it do?" asked Papa. "Every machine should do some kind of useful work."

Papa could see that Eddie was hurt. Gently he placed his arm across Eddie's shoulders and said, "Every machine should have a purpose, son, like the pile driver which I'm using down at the bridge. It's just a simple tool, but it drives the poles deep into the river bed to form a foundation for the bridge."

Eddie blinked. "Yes, I understand," he said.

"You have a great imagination, son, and I'm

proud of you," added Papa. "Just put your imagination to work for some useful purpose, like those Wright brothers over in Dayton, Ohio. They claim to be building a new-fangled machine that will take off and fly through the air like a bird. People say they're crazy, but someday they'll really succeed."

Eddie straightened up. "Oh, golly, Papa," he said, "do you really think so?"

"Ach, you're lucky to be growing up at this time, Eddie," said Papa. "Many new tools and new machines are in the making. Maybe you can have a hand in building or using them."

"I'll try, Papa," said Eddie. Immediately he started to take apart his machine.

"Now I must go to work," said Papa, starting to walk away. "Good night, Eddie."

That was the last time Eddie ever heard his father's voice. Later that same night a workman knocked at the door of the Rickenbacker home. Mary went to the door to talk with him. "Your father has been seriously hurt and has been taken to the hospital," he said. "Please let me speak with your mother."

Chapter 9

Young Head of the Family

Mama came home from the hospital with tears streaming down her pale cheeks. "Papa was hit on the head by a swinging timber," she said. "He was hurt so badly that the doctors are afraid they can't save him."

The children began to cry. "Let's not give up hope," said Eddie, holding his mother's hand. "Maybe he'll get well."

"I don't know," said Mama, closing her eyes. "All depends on God's will."

Papa died later in the summer. His death was a great shock to Mama and all seven children. The Rickenbackers had been a close-knit family and Papa had been a good husband and father. Now Mama wanted the children to look nice for their father's funeral, so she went into debt to buy new black clothes for them to wear.

After the funeral, she asked the children to gather in the kitchen. "I want you to promise to help one another in the years to come," she said. "Some of you will be more successful than others and some of you will have more money than others. Always be ready and willing to share with a brother or sister who may be in need."

That night when Eddie went to bed, he couldn't sleep. He tossed and turned and finally crept out of bed and went down to the kitchen. There he found his mother sitting at the table with her face in her hands. "Mama," he said, "I was hoping I would find you here. From now on I want to help you in every possible way. I promise never to cause you any more trouble again."

Mama reached out her hand to pat him, and he sat down across from her at the table. For a while they sat silently, but soon Eddie realized that he was sitting in Papa's chair at the table. "Maybe this is where I belong," he thought. "Now that I'm nearly fourteen years old, I should take Papa's place, and be head of the family."

After he went back to bed, he lay awake all night thinking. He knew that more than anything else, Mama needed money. If he was going to be head of the family, he must quit school and find a full-time job.

The next morning he left home as usual, but instead of stopping at school he headed for the Federal Glass Factory two miles away. He thought that he might get a job there because his brother Bill had worked there. Inside the office, a man asked him how old he was. "I'm nearly fourteen," he replied.

"Well, you look mighty skinny for a boy of that age," said the man. "Do you really need to get a job?"

"Yes," replied Eddie. "My father just died and I have to go to work to help support the family. I promise to work hard."

"All right," said the man. "I'll put you on the night shift. You'll work from six o'clock in the evening until six o'clock in the morning six days a week. Come back at six o'clock tonight to start."

"I'll be here," said Eddie grimly.

From the glass factory he went directly home to tell his mother. "Mama," he said seriously, "I have decided to quit school and go to work to help you. I've got a job working nights at the glass factory."

"Oh, no!" cried Mama, shaking her head. "I can't let you do that. You must keep on going to school and wait until you're older to take a job."

Eddie pleaded with her. "Mama, I want to be head of the family," he said. "Let me work to help earn money."

Mama kept objecting but finally agreed. "All right, Eddie," she said. "I really don't know what I would do without you."

That evening Eddie did the chores early and walked to the glass factory in time to start to work at six o'clock. He was assigned to a group to help make glass tumblers. All night long he carried trays of newly shaped tumblers to be baked in a fiery-hot oven.

When morning came, he was so exhausted that he could hardly drag himself home. While he was eating breakfast, he slumped in his chair and fell sound asleep. "Poor boy," said his mother, "he's even too tired to eat."

At the end of his first week, he proudly carried his pay envelope home to Mama. Inside the envelope there were three dollars and fifty cents, which was more money than he had ever seen before. "Thank you, Eddie," said Mama. "You certainly are a good boy."

Eddie also tried to keep on doing his chores at home. He looked after the goats and chickens, delivered the milk, and brought fuel and water to the kitchen. Before long he decided to look for a daytime job so he could sleep nights rather than days. He found a job in a foundry, where he earned six dollars a week.

The family was now doing very well. Three children—Bill, Mary, and Eddie—were working to help support the family. Eddie constantly looked for jobs where he could earn more money. One summer afternoon when he was nearly fifteen years old, he walked downtown. At a busy intersection he noticed that a crowd of people were watching something on the street. He discovered that they were watching a man demonstrate a new automobile.

It was a two-passenger Ford runabout, called a Model C Turtleback. It had fancy fenders over the wheels and brass headlights. Strangely it had a wheel for guiding it instead of a long bar. Most surprising of all, its engine was up front under a hood instead of under the seat.

Early automobiles like this one often had trouble. Often they wouldn't start, broke down, or got stuck in the mud. Mostly they could only be used in summer when the weather was warm.

The crowd listened quietly while the man demonstrated the new Ford runabout. Finally somebody called out, "How strong is its engine and how much does it cost?"

"It has an eight-horsepower gasoline engine," replied the man, "and it sells for $500, which you can see is a real bargain."

"I'd rather have a horse," replied the questioner

"All right, kid," he said. "Hop in and I'll take
you for a ride."

as somebody began to whistle the new song, "In My
Merry Oldsmobile."

Eddie stepped into the street to look closely at
the shiny new runabout. He remembered what his
father had said about the future of horseless carriages: "Everybody will have one some day." Eddie

boldly called out to the man who was demonstrating the new horseless carriage, "Say, Mister, do you ever take people for rides in your car? I would like to go for a ride."

The man pushed back his brown derby hat and looked at Eddie in surprise. Finally he decided that he had a chance to demonstrate that a young boy wasn't afraid to go for a ride. "All right, kid," he said. "Hop in and I'll take you for a ride."

Shaking with excitement, Eddie climbed into the shiny runabout. The man adjusted a lever in the steering wheel and went around to the front of the car to crank the engine, but nothing happened. "Get a horse to pull it," shouted a man in the crowd.

Suddenly the engine let out a sputter, followed by a mighty roar that frightened everybody. Hurriedly the man climbed beside Eddie and grabbed the steering wheel. Then the automobile took off with a jerk and traveled along the streets at the exciting speed of ten miles an hour.

Eddie felt as if he was in another world. "How lucky I am," he thought as he clutched the thick leather seat. "Not one boy in a million has ever ridden in a horseless carriage."

The man drove the new Ford several times around the block and finally let Eddie out in front of the crowd. "Thank you, mister," said Eddie as he hopped down to the street. "That was great."

From then on, Eddie wanted to become a mechanic so he could work on engines. He decided to apply for a job at the nearby Pennsylvania Railroad Shops, where men repaired railroad cars and locomotives. There he could learn to become a mechanic.

Chapter 10

From Mechanic to Auto Racer

Eddie quickly got a job as an apprentice mechanic in the Pennsylvania Railroad shops. He enjoyed his work and learning about machines. After a few weeks, however, he injured his leg and had to stay at home for a few days.

One afternoon while he was recovering, he limped down the street for exercise. Soon he came to an old run-down building with a sign in front which read, "Evans Garage. Bicycle and Automobile Repairs." He peeked through the dusty front window and saw some automobiles standing inside the building. Suddenly he decided, "I should like to work here where I can learn about automobiles."

He stepped inside and found a man lying on his back under one of the automobiles. "Hey, Mister," he called. "Are you Mr. Evans?"

The man wriggled his legs and slid out from under the automobile. "Yes, but I'm mighty busy right now," he said. "What do you want?"

"I'm looking for a job," replied Eddie.

Mr. Evans rubbed his face and left a streak of grease on his cheek. "Well, I could use a boy to keep the place clean and to look after things when I'm away," he said.

"That sounds exactly like what I want," cried Eddie. "Mostly I want to learn about automobiles and their engines."

Eddie had a new job, and as he had hoped, he learned many things about automobiles. He learned how to repair gasoline engines. He learned how to repair motors and charge batteries for electric automobiles. He even learned how to drive automobiles forward and backward a few feet inside the garage.

From time to time he told the members of his family and some of his neighborhood friends about driving automobiles. Some of them were amazed and others didn't believe him. "We don't see you driving anywhere along the streets," they chided him.

Before long Mr. Evans left Eddie in charge of the garage while he made a short trip away from the city. Eagerly Eddie looked at the Waverly Electric which was stored in the garage. "Now will be a good time to show everybody that I can really drive," he said to himself.

Promptly he started the motor and drove the electric car out into the street. At first he felt a little nervous guiding it in and out of the slow-moving traffic. By the time he got home, however, he felt sure of himself. He swung down proudly from the high seat and strode into the kitchen. "Mama," he called, "I have an electric automobile out front. Let me take you for a ride."

Mama was startled. She put on a coat and fastened her hat tightly on her head. Then, half-afraid, she walked out to the street and climbed into the small car.

By now the neighbors were coming out to see young redheaded Eddie Rickenbacker taking his mother for a ride in a fancy automobile. He drove about the neighborhood at the high speed of ten miles per hour. "Please don't drive so fast, Eddie," cried his mother, waving proudly to one of her neighbors.

When Eddie stopped to let out his mother, he found a crowd of people waiting. They asked many questions about the electric automobile and were surprised by how much he knew. Never had he felt more important.

Not long after that, he met one of his old Horsehead friends. Eddie and his friend talked and laughed about some of the good times they had had together. Finally the friend said, "I hear you've been working in a garage."

"Yes," said Eddie, half ashamed. "Are you still going to high school?"

"Yes, and I'm going to keep going until I graduate," replied his friend.

"You're certainly lucky to be able to get an education," said Eddie. "I wish I had gone to high school."

This conversation made Eddie wonder if he still should try to go back to school. He talked about it with one of his former teachers. "It might be better for you to take a correspondence or home-study course," said the teacher. "I'll give you the names of several schools that offer correspondence courses so you can write to them."

Eddie was most interested in a course in mechanical engineering, which would include special instruction on gasoline engines. He investigated all the schools his former teacher had suggested before choosing one. He studied the lessons the school sent him in all his spare moments.

About this time more automobile companies were springing up. One was the Frayer-Miller Company, which was near the Evans Garage. One of the owners, Lee Frayer, regularly worked at the factory every Sunday, and Eddie started to go to the factory to watch.

After a few Sundays Mr. Frayer called to him. "Hey, boy, who are you and what do you want?"

"My name is Eddie Rickenbacker," replied Eddie, "and I would like a job helping to build automobiles here in your plant."

Mr. Frayer shook his head. "You're too young to help build automobiles," he said. "There's nothing you can do around here."

Eddie didn't give up easily. He saw piles of trash and dirt scattered around the main room of the plant. "Mr. Frayer," he said, "you're mistaken. I can see a job here for me. I'll come early in the morning and hope you like what you find I have done."

Early the next morning he went to the building and hunted up a shovel and broom. Then he started at one end of the room, hoping to finish his cleaning before Mr. Frayer arrived. Before long, Mr. Frayer came in and was surprised to find Eddie there. "What are you doing here?" he asked.

"I'm cleaning the room to show you that there's work here for me to do," replied Eddie. "How do you like what I've done?"

Mr. Frayer stared in amazement at the clean end of the room and frowned as he glanced at the dirty end. "I like what you have done, and you have won yourself a job," he replied. "Finish your cleaning and I'll put you to work in the factory."

First he placed Eddie in the tool-making department to help make and assemble carburetors for gasoline engines. Later one afternoon while Eddie was studying his correspondence lesson, he stopped to talk with him. "I can see you want to get ahead," he said. "I'm transferring you to our engineering department."

Eddie was delighted. Now he would have a chance to draw and design various parts for automobiles. The company built only one gasoline automobile a month, but now it was building three little racing cars to enter the 1906 Vanderbilt Cup Races on Long Island, New York. Many workers were excited about these races, which were to be held on Long Island in September. One of them explained the races to Eddie. "They were started by William K. Vanderbilt, Jr., a wealthy sportsman," he said. "So far French cars have won every year, but this year we hope that some American car will win. If one of our Frayer-Miller racers can win, it will help to make our company famous."

In September Eddie went to the railroad yards to help load the three racers on a freight train. As he worked, Mr. Frayer came up to him. "I plan to drive one of these cars myself," he said. "How

Mr. Frayer handed Eddie some racing goggles and a leather helmet. He explained exactly what he wanted Eddie to do during the race.

would you like to go along to be my mechanic?"

"Oh, sure!" cried Eddie, caught by surprise. "Of course I would like to go."

When they reached the racetrack, Mr. Frayer handed Eddie some racing goggles and a leather helmet. He explained exactly what he wanted Eddie to do during the race. "If the oil pressure falls, be ready to use a hand pump to force oil into the engine. Watch the tires to make sure they aren't beginning to show signs of wear. And last of all tap me on the knee when somebody wishes to go around us."

Eddie listened and repeated what he had heard to show that he understood what to do. The race, which was to be 300 miles long, was held on a stretch of dirt road. Only five cars from each country could enter. Trials were held first to select the five American cars.

On the day of the trials, Eddie excitedly sat beside Mr. Frayer, waiting for the signal to start. Their car took off like a streak and jumped into the lead. "We're going to win!" shouted Eddie. "We're going to win!"

Almost at once the engine began to heat up and to pound. Mr. Frayer had to slow down and pull off to the side of the road. "Well, I guess we're through," he said calmly.

Later that day Mr. Frayer's other two racers also lost out because of engine trouble. Much to Eddie's surprise, he neither flew into a rage nor shed tears over the matter. His calmness led Eddie to adopt the following motto for life, "Try hard to win, but don't cry if you lose."

In 1907 both Mr. Frayer and Eddie joined the

Columbus Buggy Company, which now was manufacturing automobiles. After working in the factory for a couple of years, Eddie began to demonstrate and sell automobiles for the company in Texas and several other states. One day the company sent him a new sports car. This new car had a left-hand drive, the first ever built in America.

Eddie painted the car white and made minor improvements to the engine. Then he decided to drive it in auto races being held at state and county fairs across the country. In his first race he had a wreck, but he repaired the car and went on to win many races.

In the spring of 1911, Mr. Frayer called him back to Columbus. "I have a new race car, my Red Wing Special, which I'm going to enter in the new 500-Mile race at the Indianapolis Motor Speedway on Memorial Day," he said. "I want you to go to Indianapolis with me and help me drive it in the race."

"Thanks!" cried Eddie. "Of course I'll go."

On Memorial Day they entered the Red Wing Special in the Indianapolis race against some of the most powerful cars ever made. They had to settle for eleventh place, but by now Eddie knew racing was what he wanted to do.

Chapter 11

Speed King in Auto Racing

On Memorial Day the following year, young Eddie Rickenbacker went back to the Indianapolis Motor Speedway to race again. This time he was going to drive the Red Wing Special himself with a mechanic riding beside him. Each car had to make 200 laps, or trips around the two-and-one-half mile track, to complete the race. Twenty-four cars were racing.

The race was supposed to start at ten o'clock in the morning. Long before daylight, however, crowds of people started to come. They came in automobiles and horse-drawn buggies and wagons. Some rode horseback. Shortly before ten o'clock the band began to play, "Everybody's Doing it Now," and the crowd started to clap and cheer. The drivers and mechanics pushed their cars out to their starting

Long before daylight, however, crowds of people started to come. They came in automobiles and horse-drawn buggies and wagons. Some rode horseback.

positions on the track. Soon all the cars took off for a slow drive of one lap around the track. Then officials dropped a flag to signal that the race was on.

Eddie pushed his foot hard against the accelera-

tor, making his car surge forward. He rode through a cloud of smoke as cars passed one another, trying to get better positions in the race. He caught the odor of burning rubber as the tires screeched at high speed along the track.

At the end of fifty-five laps, when he was in fourth place, his engine broke down and he had to quit the race. "This isn't my lucky day," he said, wiping the dust from his face, "but I'll win next year."

By now Eddie was so interested in auto racing that he decided to give up his job demonstrating and selling automobiles to race full time. He went to Des Moines, Iowa, to see Fred Duesenberg, a noted car designer. When he arrived, he found Duesenberg working on three cars to enter the May 1913 race at Indianapolis. "I'd like a job driving cars," he explained.

"I need mechanics, not drivers," replied Duesenberg. "I'll pay you three dollars a day to work for us as a mechanic."

Eddie swallowed hard. This was only about half as much as he had earned as an automobile demonstrator and salesman. "I'll do it," he said, ready to take a chance.

For many long months he and other mechanics worked on the three racecars, called Masons. In the race at Indianapolis, Duesenberg failed to win. Later Eddie drove in several smaller races, some of which he won.

The next big race in which Duesenberg entered his racecars was a 300-mile race at Sioux City, Iowa, in July 1913. He asked Eddie to drive one of the cars and put him in charge of the Duesenberg racing team. Before the race Eddie and the others had a total of seven dollars in their pockets. They knew they had to do well, or quit. The racetrack was a two-mile oval made of a mixture of hard soil and rocks, called gumbo. Often during races, chunks of the gumbo broke loose and drivers constantly had to watch out for them.

The race began at noon. One by one different cars dropped out with engine trouble. One driver and his mechanic were killed in a thundering crash. Gumbo from the track flew up and struck Eddie in the face, but he kept going. His Mason and a popular new car called the Mercer took turns in the lead and sometimes ran wheel to wheel.

Suddenly Eddie noticed that his oil gauge was extremely low. He nudged his mechanic to start pumping oil by hand but nothing happened. The mechanic was slumped in his seat with a red lump on his forehead. He had been knocked out by a chunk of the flying gumbo.

By now they had only four more laps to go. The engine was beginning to smoke from lack of oil, but Eddie knew that he must keep going. "I just have to win," he thought, "even if the engine burns up."

At the beginning of the final lap, his engine was red-hot and pounding loudly. The Mercer was right behind him, ready to take the lead. Fortunately, the engine kept going and Eddie won the race.

After he crossed the finish line, one of his tires exploded, but now he didn't care. He turned and saw one of his teammates, who was driving another Mason, come in third. He jumped out happily and ran over to congratulate him. At the same time, his mechanic came to and joined the celebration.

Eddie collected over $10,000 for winning the race, and his teammate collected $2,500 for coming in third. For several minutes they stood patting one another joyfully. "Now we're rich," they cried.

Late that day Eddie sent a telegram to his mother in Columbus, Ohio. His telegram read, "You can believe what you read in the newspapers about me."

Winning this race made him a national racing hero. He now wanted to drive and learn about other racing cars. He joined a team driving Maxwell cars and won races from coast to coast. He constantly experimented with new parts for his cars. In Rhode Island, for instance, he won a race for $10,000 by using extra-heavy tires that wouldn't blow out.

Eddie knew that auto racing required both strength and skill. He watched his diet carefully and obtained plenty of rest. He wrote a book of instructions to help his mechanics achieve greater skill. They improved until they could replace wheels or make other similar repairs in only a few seconds.

He saw an airplane parked in a grassy field and
decided to stop and look at it.

Sometimes the seconds they saved made the differ-
ence between winning and losing a race.

In 1915 Eddie organized his own racing team.
By the end of 1916 he ranked third among racers in
the country, after winning $60,000 in prize money
during the year.

One day in November when he was in California
for a race, he took a short drive into the country.
He saw an airplane parked in a grassy field and
decided to stop and look at it.

He drove into the field and pulled up at a small
airplane hangar. A young man came out and
shook his hand. "Hi, Eddie Rickenbacker," he
said. "I'm Glenn Martin. I recognized you from

your picture in newspapers. What brings you here?"

"If I could, I'd like to look over your airplane," Eddie replied.

Martin explained that he had been flying airplanes for a number of years. Now he owned a small company nearby and was building small "bombers" for the United States Navy. Each bomber had a front seat for the pilot and another directly behind it for the gunner.

Eddie looked over the bomber with great interest. "Would you like to take a ride?" asked Martin.

"Sure," replied Eddie, excited because this would be his first airplane ride. He climbed happily into the gunner's seat behind Martin. The airplane took off; he leaned back in his seat, and felt that flying was wonderful.

All his life he had been dizzy when he looked down from high buildings, but he wasn't dizzy at all. Afterwards he asked Martin, "Why wasn't I dizzy up in the air?"

"Because you had no edge to look over," replied Martin. "You had no way of judging how far you were from the ground."

Eddie was now one of the most popular and widely known auto racers in America. People admired him both for making important improvements in his cars and for his careful driving. He had never had a serious accident in all his racing.

At this time World War I was in progress in Europe, with Germany waging war against a group of countries, including England and France, called the Allies. Because of this war, auto racing in Europe had stopped. The Sunbeam Motor Company of England invited Eddie to come to England in 1916 to design a new car to enter in races for them in the United States.

In December he took off by ship for England, and arrived safely despite the danger of German submarines to ships crossing the Atlantic Ocean. At once he began designing a new racing car that would do 125 miles an hour. For a time, because of his German name, some English officials suspected him of being a spy. The suspicion amused and angered him. At the Sunbeam plant he met English pilots who were flying airplanes over the war front in France. "We need better airplanes," they said. "We're fighting the war with our backs against the wall."

Eddie felt sorry for them. "Maybe I can learn to fly and help them," he thought.

In February 1917, he received a telephone call from a friend urging him to come home.

"The United States is breaking off relations with Germany," explained his friend. "Start home at once, because Germany has announced that within five days her submarines will begin to attack American ships."

Eddie left England immediately. On the way home he thought about the problem the United States would have trying to build up an air force. He decided to offer to organize a squadron made up of his auto racing friends.

When he presented his idea to the Army Signal Corps, the general and his staff turned him down. They looked at him and said, "None of you have a college education. Besides, most of you are too old to fly."

In April the United States entered the war. Eddie now returned to auto racing. He hoped to enter the next race at the Indianapolis Motor Speedway, but this race was called off because of the war. Then suddenly he received a long distance telephone call that led to great changes in his life.

Chapter 12

Flying Ace in World War I

"How would you like to go to Europe as an Army staff automobile driver?" asked Major Lewis by long distance telephone. He was a friend of Eddie's, now at Army staff headquarters in Washington D.C.

"Right now it sounds wonderful," replied Eddie, "but let me think it over."

That night he lay awake, thinking about this surprising offer. Finally he decided to accept, hoping that somehow he might get an opportunity to become a flyer. In Europe he was soon driving a staff car for Colonel William "Billy" Mitchell. A short time later he asked Colonel Mitchell to be transferred to some form of air service, but the Colonel simply said, "Forget it. Forget it."

Eddie kept watching for an opportunity to learn

to fly. Soon he met an old friend, Captain James Miller, who was in charge of building a base for a flying school at Issoudun, outside of Paris. Captain Miller offered him a job as chief engineering officer at the new base, and agreed to let him take flying lessons. The Captain asked Colonel Mitchell to transfer Eddie, and this time the Colonel let him go. Eddie went to the Tours flying school and earned his wings and the bars of a first lieutenant. Then he reported to the Issoudun field to start his new post.

As chief engineering officer at the base, he selected and purchased tools and equipment for the machine shops and maintenance crews. He had to work night and day to get the machine shops ready in time for the first flying students to arrive.

After Eddie learned to fly, he wanted to get combat training. Whenever possible he practiced doing the tailspin, loop, and other necessary maneuvers for combat flying. As a final step, he attended a gunnery school.

In March 1918, he joined the 94th Aero Pursuit Squadron. This squadron, which included twenty pilots and about sixty mechanics, was the first all-American unit ready for combat. It was stationed near Villeneuve, about fifteen miles behind the front lines.

The chief trainer for the Squadron was Major Raoul Lufbery. He had flown for several years with the French Air Force before the United States entered the war. The pilots listened to Luf carefully because he had won many air victories. "When you're on patrol see everything possible," he said. "When you're engaged in an air battle, find the enemy's weakest spot."

As Luf sized up his pilots, he picked out Eddie as one of the best. He chose him and Lieutenant Douglas Campbell to fly with him in the squadron's first patrol over German lines. "Look out for Archie, the German's anti-aircraft fire," warned their fellow pilots.

Luf and the two other pilots walked out to their wooden-framed, unarmed airplanes. They put on their fur-lined flying suits, pulled down their fur-lined leather helmets, and climbed into their seats. Excitedly they adjusted their flying goggles and waited for the mechanics to spin their propellers. Then, with a roar, they took off.

They rose to a height of 15,000 feet and crossed the front lines between Rheims and Verdun. As Eddie looked down, he was shocked to see so much barren land. He couldn't even see a tree left standing after three years of war.

Suddenly his airplane rocked from the blast of a

German shell, which burst nearby. At once shells started to burst all around him, giving out puffs of black smoke. He realized that these shells were coming from a German anti-aircraft battery far below. He soon learned to adjust his airplane to the blasts of the shells. In fact, he began to enjoy this contest of wits with the anti-aircraft gunners.

The other pilots and the mechanics were waiting when Major Lufbery and his two companions taxied back to the hangers. "Did Archie bother you?" they asked. "Did you see any enemy airplanes?"

"No, we saw only shells bursting around us," said Eddie.

Major Lufbery chuckled. "I'm sorry to contradict you," he said, "but three groups of enemy airplanes were flying about us."

The major strode over and pointed out holes in the wings and tail of Eddie's airplane, only a few feet from where he had been seated. "Good grief," exclaimed Eddie, turning pale. "I could have been killed!"

During the following weeks, the squadron received a supply of guns for the pilots to carry on their single-seated airplanes. Eddie took part in many air battles. On April 29 while he was engaged in combat, he downed his first enemy airplane. Now he really felt that he was making progress.

One of Eddie's closest calls came about a month later. At four o'clock one morning, he and another pilot took off in separate airplanes to watch for German airplanes coming across the lines. Before long, he sighted three Albatros airplanes taking off from a German airfield. Silently he climbed to a height of about 20,000 feet, and then swooped down after them with his guns blasting away. He hit one of the airplanes, causing it to explode and fall to the ground in flames.

The other two Albatros airplanes now turned to attack him. Quickly he shifted his airplane out of a steep dive to climb upward again. This sudden change caused the wind to tear the linen cloth loose from his upper right wing, and his airplane went into a tailspin. Repeatedly he tried to right it, but it only fell faster and faster. Meanwhile the two German Albatros airplanes kept firing at him. "Oh God," he prayed, "get me out of this."

Desperately he jerked on the controls one last time and miraculously the airplane righted itself and started to wobble forward. Now he hoped only to keep it in the air long enough to get back to the American lines two miles away. He succeeded and was even able to land safely on his own airfield.

When Eddie stepped from the airplane, his knees wobbled but he felt proud and happy. The other pilots crowded around, eager to shake his hand and hear his story. All now realized that he was one of the best and bravest flyers in their group.

By now the airplanes which the 94th Squadron used had become badly worn. The government arranged to replace them with new airplanes, called Spads, from a French airplane company. After the pilots heard this news, they could hardly wait to get them.

On the Fourth of July Eddie went to Paris to join other Americans in celebrating our national birthday. While he was there, he visited an American supply depot at Orly, on the outskirts of Paris. As he looked around he spotted three new Spad airplanes ready for his squadron. He examined one which had the numeral "1" painted on its side. "Is this Spad ready to fly?" he asked with a broad grin.

"Yes, Rick," replied the officer, using Eddie's new nickname.

"Then why not let me fly it over to the base?" asked Eddie.

"All right," agreed the officer.

Eddie happily flew the new Spad to his air base at Touquin and demonstrated it to the other pilots. In September the Allied forces launched a furious combined air and ground attack against the Germans at Saint Mihiel, France. All the air

Quickly he swung down and shot a Fokker,
causing it to fall.

squadrons were ordered to fly around the clock, to shoot down airplanes and to attack supply trains.

One day when Eddie was making an observation flight, he spotted four crack German airplanes, called Fokkers, chasing several American airplanes. Quickly he swung down and shot a Fokker, causing it to fall. At once the other three Fokkers, all of which had red noses, turned to attack him. "Golly!" he cried. "They're part of the famous 'Flying Circus!'"

The Fokker planes zoomed, sideslipped, and corkscrewed through the clear sky. Eddie had to do some very skillful flying in order to keep away from them. "I've never seen such flying in my life," he thought with a chill. "How can I escape them?"

Soon he saw a hole beneath him and went into a straight dive. Then he leveled off, opened up his throttle, and pulled away, leaving the three Fokkers behind him. "What a miraculous escape," he thought.

The following day he had another fight with the Flying Circus and hit one Fokker. Now he had shot down a total of seven airplanes, and was give the title "American Ace of Aces." Back home his mother was very proud of his receiving this honor. She had just written urging him to fly slowly and close to the ground.

Soon the Allies won a smashing victory at Saint Mihiel. For the first time in history, airplanes had played a prominent part in winning a major victory. American pilots had flown far behind the German lines and caused thousand of soldiers to surrender.

Eddie was now made Commanding Officer of the 94th Squadron. He gave his men strict orders about taking care of their engines and guns. "We have a big job to do," he told them, "and we'll work together as equals. There'll be no saluting around here. I'll fly along with the rest of you."

Early the next morning Eddie took off alone on patrol duty over the battlefront at Verdun. Far away he spotted two German picture-taking airplanes headed for the Allied lines. Directly above them were five red-nosed Fokker airplanes serving as a guard. He waited high in the sky until the seven airplanes flew by below him. Then he dove down silently and shot down one of the five Fokker planes. The four others split off but made no attempt to fight back.

A few minutes later he swooped down to attack one of the two photographic planes. As he came near, one of them shot at him and the other circled to attack him in the rear. The three planes went round and round, with Eddie watching for a chance to strike. Suddenly he shifted his position and shot down one of the planes.

The four Fokkers now came swooping down toward him, but he streaked for home base as fast as he could go. "Well done, Rick!" shouted the other pilots, rushing out to greet him. "You've had two victories before breakfast."

For taking part in this battle he later was granted the Congressional Medal of Honor, our nation's highest award for military service. By the end of October he had won twenty-six victories in 134 air battles, more than any other American pilot. His 94th Squadron also ranked first, having shot down sixty-nine airplanes and balloons.

On November 10, 1918, while he was talking with his pilots about the next day's mission, he received a telephone call. "Captain," cried a voice, "we have just learned at headquarters that the war will end at eleven o'clock tomorrow morning. Call off future missions."

Grinning broadly, Eddie dropped the phone and turned to inform his pilots. "The war will end at eleven o'clock tomorrow morning," he announced. "All future missions are called off."

Moments later the anti-aircraft batteries began to shoot shells into the air to celebrate the end of the fighting. The pilots from all the squadrons gathered and built a big bonfire. They

Then the enemy soldiers tossed their helmets into the
air and ran out on the quiet battlefield to
embrace one another.

talked happily and sang songs.

Shortly before eleven o'clock the following
morning, Eddie made one last flight over the
German lines. At five minutes to eleven the

Germans fired at him. Then at eleven they stopped firing and threw their guns on the ground.

Promptly at eleven o'clock both the German and Allied bases shot shells and flares into the air to announce that the war was over. Then the enemy soldiers tossed their helmets into the air and ran out on the quiet battlefield to embrace one another. World War I was over, and Eddie Rickenbacker could go home.

What Happened Next?

• The United States awarded the Medal of Honor, the nation's highest military award, to Eddie Rickenbacker for his 26 victories over German warplanes during World War I.

• Eddie Rickenbacker drove in the first Indianapolis 500 Mile Race in 1911. In 1927, he bought the Indianapolis Motor Speedway for $700,000. During the twenty years that he owned it, he helped to make it the famous racecourse that it is today.

• In 1938, Eddie purchased Eastern Air Lines and remained Chairman of the Board until the company merged with Trans World Airlines in 1963.

• In 1942, while on a secret mission for the government, the plane carrying Eddie and several others crashed into the Pacific Ocean. They were lost at sea for 24 days before the Navy rescued them.

• Eddie Rickenbacker was the father of two sons, David and William.

When Eddie Rickenbacker Lived

Date	Event
1890	Eddie Rickenbacker was born in Columbus, Ohio on October 8.
1891–1913	Eddie grew up and started working following the death of his father.
1913–1918	Eddie became a famous racedriver and Ace pilot in World War I.
1918–1942	Promoting the sport of auto racing and flying, Eddie later became president of Eastern Airlines.
1942–1973	Eddie carried out missions in World War II and then gradually retired.
1973	Eddie Rickenbacker died in Zurich, Switzerland on July 23.

Fun Facts About
Eddie Rickenbacker

• The "Rickenbacker" car, manufactured in 1927 by Eddie's company, the Rickenbacker Motor Company, was the first medium-priced American car with brakes on all four wheels.

• When Eddie first started flying, he was often airsick.

• When the plane carrying Eddie on a government mission crashed into the ocean, the surviving men had only enough food for three days. They were in danger of starving when on the eighth day, a seagull landed on Eddie's head. The bird became a source of food and fish bait that allowed them to live until they were rescued.

• Eddie Rickenbacker said, "Courage is doing what you're afraid to do. There can be no courage unless you're scared."

• The Eddie Rickenbacker postage stamp was issued on September 25, 1995

Visit "http://www.patriapress.com/rickenbacker" to learn more about Eddie Rickenbacker.

About the Author

"My message is love of country and I think we ought to appreciate what we've got," observed Kathryn Sisson. "No country on earth has what we have." Newspaper reporter, publicist and author of numerous articles and books, Mrs. Sisson was a lifelong member and Vice Regent of the Boca Raton Chapter of the Daughters of the American Revolution. She served as a vice president of the National League of American Penwomen, and was a member of the Women's National Book Association, Society of Midland Authors and the Children's Reading Round Table of Chicago. Children's books penned include *Black Hawk, Young Sauk Warrior, John Hancock, New England Boy* and *Famous American Patriots for Young People,* which earned Mrs. Sisson the Dolly Madison Award from the Sons of the American Revolution